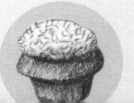

Little Elliot
BIG CITY

For anyone who feels unnoticed

The Five Mile Press Pty Ltd
1 Centre Road, Scoresby
Victoria 3179 Australia
www.fivemile.com.au
Part of the Bonnier Publishing Group
www.bonnierpublishing.com
Copyright © 2014 by Mike Curato

First published by:
Henry Holt and Company, LLC
Publishers since 1866
175 Fifth Avenue
New York, New York 10010
mackids.com

Printed in China
5 4 3 2 1

Little Elliot
BIG CITY

by Mike Curato

The Five Mile Press

Little Elliot was an elephant.

He was different
in many ways.

Little Elliot loved living in a big city, but sometimes it was hard being so small in such a huge place.

He had to be careful not
to be stepped on.

He had trouble opening doors.

And he could never catch a cab.

Even life at home was a bit challenging.

Still, Elliot enjoyed
the little things . . .

. . . small treasures . . .

160

Speranza
BAKERY
Est. 1905

. . . and most of all, cupcakes!

One day, Elliot tried to
buy a cupcake, but no
one noticed him.

Walking home, Elliot was so sad that
he barely noticed a thing . . .

. . . until he saw someone even littler than himself,
who had an even bigger problem.

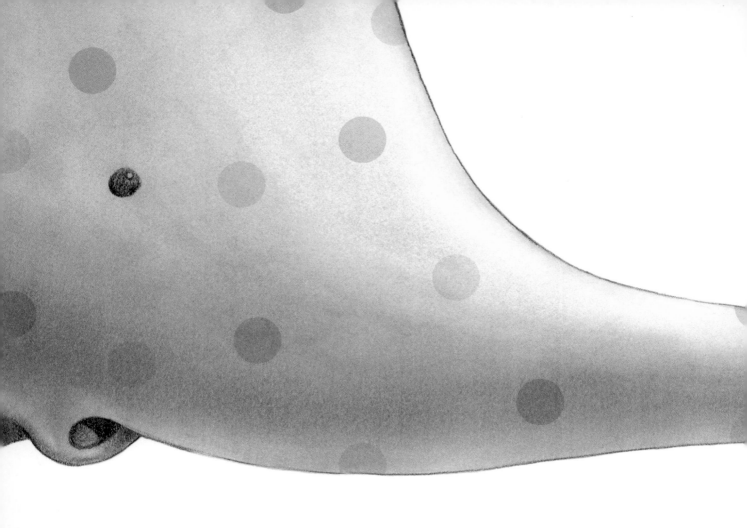

"Hello, Mouse. What is wrong?" asked Elliot.

"I'm trying to reach some food
but I'm too small," said Mouse.
"And I'm so very hungry."

"I can help!" said Elliot.

Elliot felt like the tallest elephant in the world!

The next day, Mouse came
with Elliot to the bakery.

Elliot finally
got his cupcake!

. . . and something even better.